The Little Turkle

By Deborah Van Dyken

Illustrations by Susan Mason

BLAIR

120 Morris Street
Durham, NC 27701

Book Design by Susan Mason

Library of Congress Control Number:
2018963893

ISBN 13:

978-1-949467-04-8

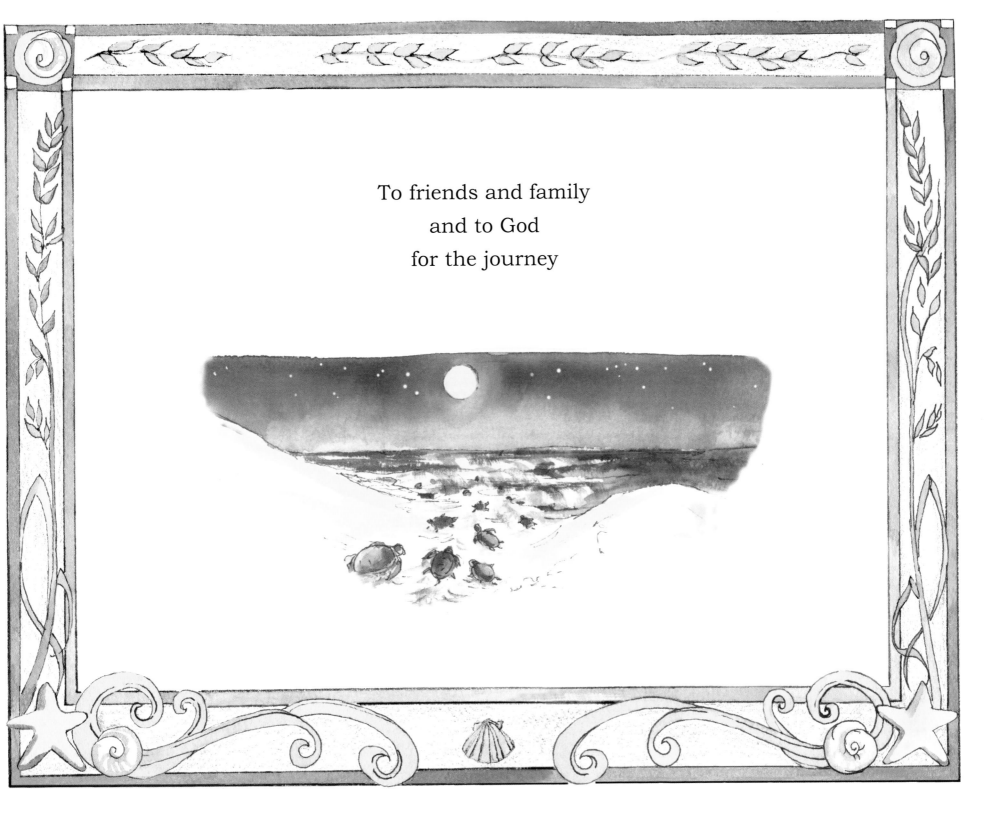

To friends and family
and to God
for the journey

Inside the egg, it was dark, and Little Turkle was sleeping. It was not time to wake up. Little Turkle slept soundly in his egg. His egg was in a nest buried deep beneath the white sand near the foaming waves of the blue ocean. Beside Little Turkle's egg, his brothers and sisters were all asleep in their eggs in the nest.

Above the nest in the salty ocean air, Little Turkle
Girl was flying. The sun was setting, and Little Turkle Girl
knew that it would soon be time for the baby turtles to wake up.

The sun set, and the sky turned from yellow, to orange, to red, to purple, and finally, to
a deep dark blue. A full golden moon rose over the dark ocean. The tide was full, and
the waves danced on the moonlit sand. It was time for Little Turkle to wake up!

Inside his egg, Little Turkle opened his brown eyes and wiggled his tiny tail. It was time to wake up! It was time to hatch!

In the dark nest, Little Turkle made a hole in his egg and crawled out of it. Beside him, his brothers and sisters came out of their eggs. Just beneath the sand, the baby turtles waited. . .

Suddenly, the baby turtles knew that it was time. They began to climb out of their nest and crawl as fast as they could across the silvery sand to the dark blue ocean. Little Turkle climbed quickly out of the warm nest. He crawled fast across the cool, wet sand. His brothers and sisters were all around him and heading towards the soft, yellow light of the moon on the ocean.

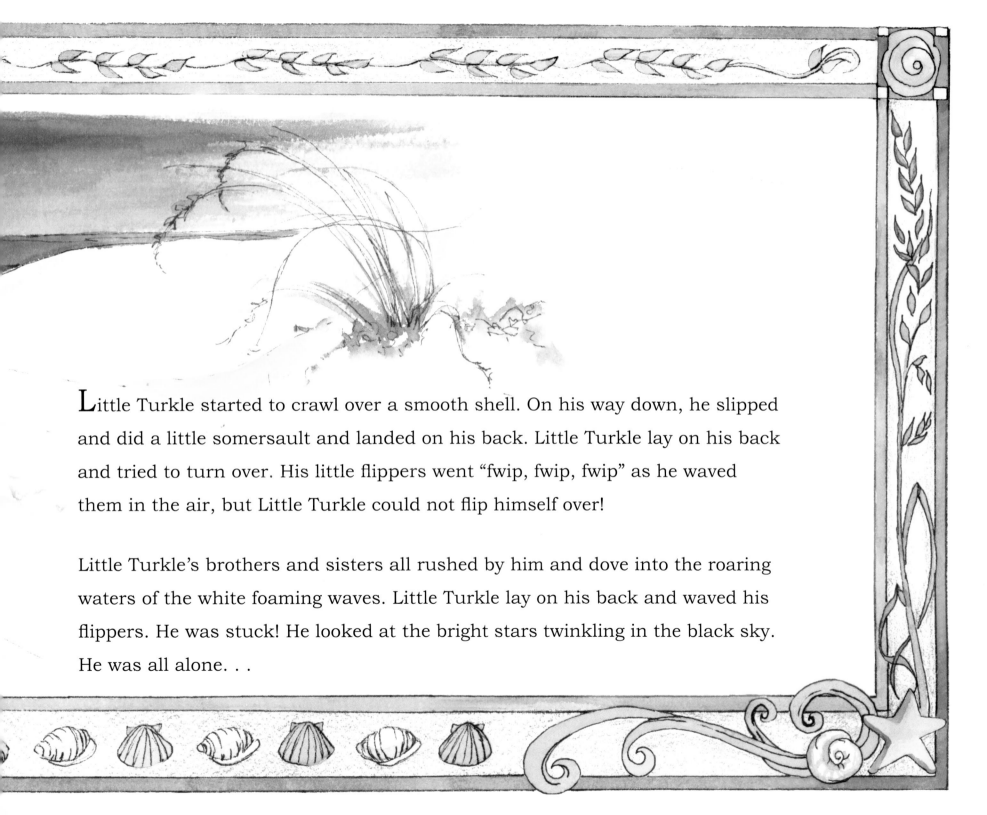

Little Turkle started to crawl over a smooth shell. On his way down, he slipped and did a little somersault and landed on his back. Little Turkle lay on his back and tried to turn over. His little flippers went "fwip, fwip, fwip" as he waved them in the air, but Little Turkle could not flip himself over!

Little Turkle's brothers and sisters all rushed by him and dove into the roaring waters of the white foaming waves. Little Turkle lay on his back and waved his flippers. He was stuck! He looked at the bright stars twinkling in the black sky. He was all alone. . .

Then, Little Turkle saw a hungry raccoon coming across a sand dune towards him. The raccoon thought that Little Turkle would make a nice bedtime snack.

Then, Little Turkle saw two pale ghost crabs coming out of their holes nearby. The ghost crabs saw Little Turkle and raised their sharp claws. They were hungry, too!

Then, Little Turkle heard the loud, harsh cries of the night birds flying over him in the dark sky. The night birds saw Little Turkle, and they were very hungry. "Help!" cried Little Turkle. "Help me! Someone please help me!"

The raccoon, the ghost crabs, and the night birds started to come closer to Little Turkle!

Overhead and down the beach, Little Turkle Girl heard Little Turkle's cries. She flew down to Little Turkle and stood beside him.

"Get back!" she said to the raccoon, the ghost crabs, and the night birds. "Get back or else!"

The raccoon, ghost crabs, and night birds stopped and looked at each other. They were very hungry, but they were not sure that they wanted to tangle with Little Turkle Girl.

Little Turkle Girl was very tiny, but she was very strong. She pushed mightily on Little Turkle's shell. Slowly but surely, Little Turkle Girl pushed Little Turkle over and back onto his flippers. Little Turkle moved his flippers in the cool sand and wiggled his tiny tail. He could crawl again!

"Let's go!" cried Little Turkle Girl. Little Turkle crawled as fast as he could to the silvery waves, and Little Turkle Girl ran right behind him. Little Turkle reached the white foaming waves and stopped. "Come with me!" said Little Turkle to Little Turkle Girl. "Okay, I will!" said Little Turkle Girl.

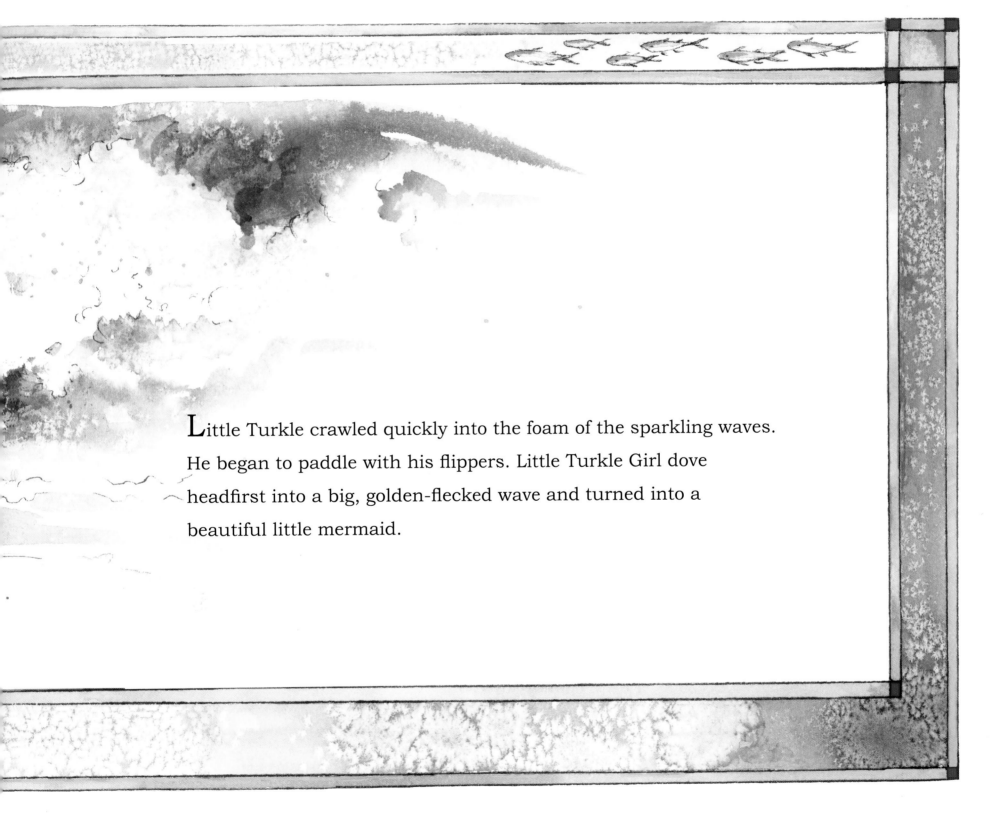

Little Turkle crawled quickly into the foam of the sparkling waves. He began to paddle with his flippers. Little Turkle Girl dove headfirst into a big, golden-flecked wave and turned into a beautiful little mermaid.

Together, Little Turkle and Little Turkle Girl
swam off into the deep blue sea where they
had many adventures and lived happily
ever after.

The End

About the Author

Deborah Van Dyken is an attorney and writer who lives in Beaufort, North Carolina, with her husband, Bill Blair, a sweet labradoodle named Rosie, a bouncy poodle mix named Pooh, and Sophie the Wonder Cat. Deborah also has two children, Charlie and Maya, and four grandchildren, Allison, Elizabeth, Catherine, and Nell.

During the past thirty years, Deborah has spent a lot of time observing sea turtles and their nests at Cape Lookout National Seashore in Carteret County, North Carolina, which inspired her to write *The Little Turkle*.

Acknowledgments

To my husband, Bill, who is the original "Little Turkle," and to the following organizations that gave me the opportunity to spend many an hour observing sea turtles and sitting by their nests: the Cape Lookout National Seashore, the National Park Service, and the North Carolina Maritime Museum.

About the Artist

Susan Mason is a native of Carteret County, North Carolina. Susan and her husband, Charles, reside in the "Down East" community of Atlantic. She has one daughter, Dawn, and two grandchildren, Peyton and Hannah.

Susan lived and taught secondary school in Arctic Alaska for 21 years. She is an artist and photographer. Susan has previously illustrated Inupiaq language books, *The Snowy Owl and the Red Fox*, and *Similes for Mother*. She was selected to paint the White House Christmas ornament for Cape Lookout National Seashore for the 2007 celebration of our national parks. Her painting "Fishin' the Pounds" was selected as the North Carolina Seafood Festival Poster for 2008. Visit her website at www.susanmasonphotoart.com.

Acknowledgments

To the people of the "Down East" communities who remember and honor how the sea has formed them and their culture. To my father, Clyde Mason, Jr., my mother, Joyce Wade Mason, my brother, Thomas C. Mason, and my sister, Pamela J. Mason, I hold dear the things you taught me about life and love.

BLAIR
120 Morris Street, Durham, NC 27701
customersupport@blairpub.com